is controlled by

This book ~~belongs to~~

For Mandy.

OXFORD
UNIVERSITY PRESS

Great Clarendon Street, Oxford OX2 6DP

Oxford University Press is a department of the University of Oxford.
It furthers the University's objective of excellence in research, scholarship, and education by publishing worldwide.

Oxford is a registered trade mark of Oxford University Press in the UK and in certain other countries

Text and illustrations © Richard Byrne 2016

The moral rights of the author/illustrator have been asserted Database right Oxford University Press (maker)

First published in 2016
This edition published in 2017

British Library Cataloguing in Publication Data
Data available

ISBN: 978-0-19-274630-6 (paperback)

10 9 8 7 6 5 4 3 2 1

Printed in China

Paper used in the production of this book is a natural, recyclableproduct made from wood grown in sustainable forests.The manufacturing process conforms to the environmental regulations of the country of origin.

Visit www.richardbyrne.co.uk

This book is out of control!

Richard BYRNE

OXFORD
UNIVERSITY PRESS

Bella was at home when someone on the other page knocked at the door.

It was Ben.
He had a new toy to show Bella.

'It's remote controlled,' said Ben.
'Watch what the ladder does
when I press the UP button.'

But nothing seemed to happen.
So Ben pressed the **SPIN**
button.

'It's just not moving!' said Bella.
'See if it will make a noise instead.'
So Ben pressed the **SIREN** button.

WOO-WOO!'

'It's a bit quiet,' said Bella.
'Try a different noise.
How about the **VOICE**
button?'

'Who said that?'
asked Bella.

'It's your dog!
He's talking!'
said Ben.

'I think TURN might work,' replied Ben.

But it didn't!
'Who's going to take control
of this book?' asked Bella.

'Oops!' said Ben.
'Well, it can't be me.'

Bella thought for a moment.
'Dear reader,' she began . . .

'it would be lovely if you could help us?'

'Try pressing the 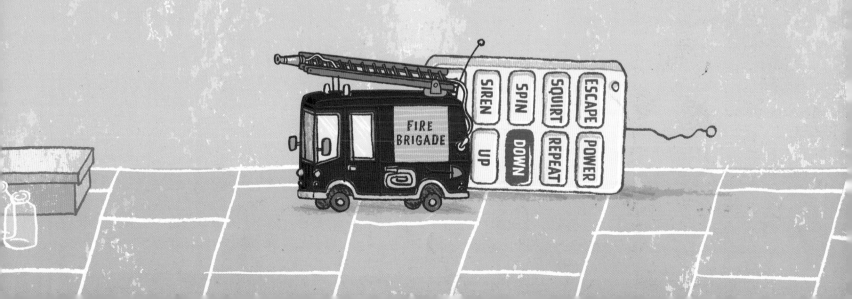 DOWN button!' suggested Ben.

'Oh no, look!' said Bella.
'Are you sure you pressed
the right button?'

Ben was starting to feel a little queasy.

'Quick!' he burbled. 'Try the ESCAPE button.'

But things became even more muddled.

Dear reader,

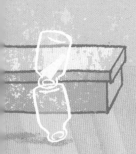

Hold on tight!
Things are about to get . . .

. . . back under control? Phew!

To make sure, Bella's dog clicked on the **UP** button.

It worked . . .

'I think your dog has found the **SQUIRT** button,' said Ben.

Dear reader,

There's one button left to press. Can you find it?

See you again soon!

Bella Ben

x x